MW01101368

The Windy Day

Halina Below

Paintings by Jacquelinne White

LESTER PUBLISHING LIMITED

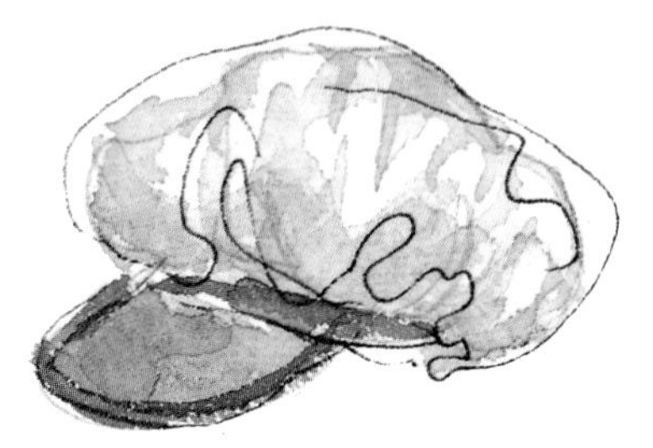

 Lester Publishing Limited acknowledges the financial assistance of the Canada Council and the Ontario Arts Council.

Canadian Cataloguing in Publication Data

Below, Halina
The windy day

ISBN 1-895555-74-4

I. White, Jacquelinne. II. Title.

PS8553.E56W56 1994 jC813'.54 C94-930667-3
PZ7.B45Wi 1994

Lester Publishing Limited
56 The Esplanade
Toronto, Ontario
Canada M5E 1A7

Design: Annabelle Stanley
Printed and bound in Hong Kong

94 95 96 97 5 4 3 2 1

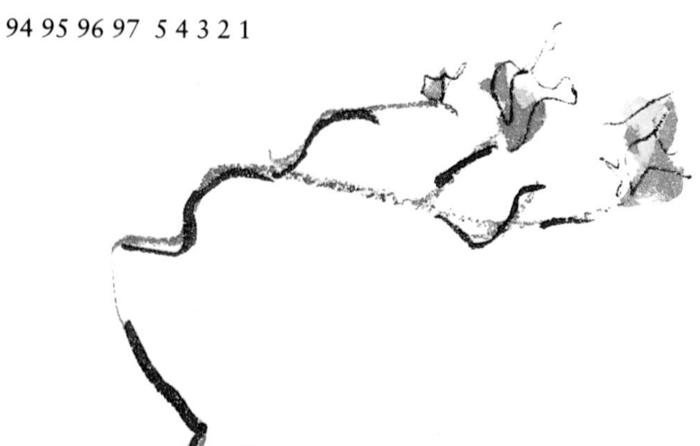

In memory of Daniel
With loving thanks to my family and special friends
H. B.

For Carla, Deven, and Ondine
J. W.

The wind had a secret.
It tugged at Thomas.
The poodle, Claude Monet,
barked at the leaves and old newspapers
as they scudded along the sidewalk.

Up, up in the air
flew Thomas's hat.
It whirled over the rooftops
and out of sight.

"Your hat!" cried Emma.
"Let's follow it," said Thomas.
"I'm flying. I'm flying," she called.
The wind lifted their voices to the clouds.

At the great grinning oak, Thomas stopped. The park filled with children as if the wind had blown them in like so many butterflies.

“Look, Emma,” said Thomas, pointing skyward.
A bright cloud had gathered there.
The children ran toward the dancing scraps of color.
“Why, it looks like hats. A cloud of hats!”

Straw hats, felt hats, a bridal veil.
Sunbonnets, toques, a busby.
Golden crowns, a crown of shells.
Hats with butterflies and birds.
A sombrero and a Haida hat.
A feather hat from Cameroon.

Hats with flowers, hats with fruit.
Hats with bows and streaming ribbons.
Why, even Thomas's hat was there!

The children laughed with delight
as they scrambled to grab the hats.

The wind teased them,
lifting the hats up, up, up to the sky
and swooping them down again.
Over and over, the children caught the hats
and the wind snatched them back.

Darkness crept through the park
as the wind swept the day away.
Mothers and fathers called their children home.
"Emma . . . Thomas . . ." Names echoed on the wind.

One by one, the children left the park.
The wind was alone with the drifting hats,
a thousand dancing shadows in the moonlight.

That night, Thomas dreamed
that the wind carried him to play in
unknown fields in a faraway land.

When morning came, the curtains hung
limply at Thomas's window.
The wind had gone,
and with it, the hats.

"What a windy day we had yesterday," said Thomas's father. "You know, I lost my favorite red baseball cap. The wind ripped it right off my head."

"How odd," said Mother. "I lost my beautiful gray straw hat the same way. I wonder where they are now?"

Thomas smiled.
He knew the secret
of the wind.